Arlington School Library

IN THE FOREST

Story and Pictures by Marie Hall Ets

Puffin Books

Penguin Books Ltd, Harmondsworth, Middlesex, England
Penguin Books, 40 West 23rd Street, New York, New York 10010, U.S.A.
Penguin Books Australia Ltd, Ringwood, Victoria, Australia
Penguin Books Canada Limited, 2801 John Street, Markham, Ontario, Canada L3R 1B4
Penguin Books (N. Z.) Ltd, 182-190 Wairau Road, Auckland 10, New Zealand

First published by The Viking Press 1944
Viking Seafarer Edition published 1970
Reprinted 1972, 1973
Published in Puffin Books 1976
Reprinted 1978, 1981, 1982, 1983, 1985 (twice)

ISBN 0 14 050.180 0
Library of Congress catalog card number: 44—7727

Printed in the United States of America
by Rae Publishing Co., Inc., Cedar Grove, New Jersey
Set in Foundry Garamond

I had a new horn and a paper hat

And I went for a walk in the forest.

A big wild lion was taking a nap,
But he woke up when he heard my horn.

"Where are you going?" he said to me.
"May I go too, if I comb my hair?"

So he combed his hair and he came too

When I went for a walk in the forest.

Two elephant babies were taking a bath,
But they stopped their splashing when they saw me.

"Wait for us," they said, as they dried their ears.

One put on his sweater. One put on some shoes.
And the elephant babies came too

When I went for a walk in the forest.

Two big brown bears sat under a tree.
They were counting their peanuts and eating jam.

"Wait a minute," they called. "We want to go too!"

So they picked up their peanuts and a spoon for the jam
And the big brown bears came too

When I went for a walk in the forest.

A mother and father kangaroo
Were teaching their baby how to hop.

"We'll bring our drums," the mother said.

"And our baby is no bother at all. I carry him in my pocket."

So the baby climbed into his mother's pouch
And the kangaroos came too

When I went for a walk in the forest.

An old gray stork was sitting down beside a pool of water.
He sat so still that I had to go near to see if he was real.

The stork stood up and looked at me. He did not say one word.
But when I went back to my animals, that funny bird came too.

Two little monkeys high up in the trees

Stopped playing and shouted when they saw me.
"A parade! A parade! We like a parade!"

So they got their best suits from a hole in a tree

And the two little monkeys came too

When I went for a walk in the forest.

I spied a rabbit behind a tall weed.

"Don't be afraid," I called to him. "If you want to go too
You can walk with me." So the rabbit came too.

I blew my horn. The lion roared. The elephants trumpeted through their trunks. The big bears growled. The kangaroos drummed. The stork clapped his bill.

The monkeys shouted and clapped their hands. But the rabbit made no noise at all—when I went for a walk in the forest.

We came to a place made for picnics and games
So we stopped and ate peanuts and jam—
And some ice cream and cake that were there.

We played Drop-the-Handkerchief once all around

And London-Bridge-Is-Falling-Down.

Then I was *It* for Hide-and-Seek, and everyone hid—
Except the rabbit. He just stood still.

"Coming!" I called. Then I opened my eyes. There wasn't an animal there at all. But there was Dad. *He* was hunting for *me*.

"Whom were you talking to?" he said.

"To my animals. They are hiding, you see."

"But it's late," Dad said. "And we must go home. Perhaps they will wait till another day."

So I called to them as I rode away. "Good-by!" I said.
"Don't go away! I'll hunt for you another day

When I come for a walk in the forest."